WHY THIS IS AN EASY READER

- This story has been carefully written to keep the young reader's interest high.

- It is told in a simple, open style, with a strong rhythm that adds enjoyment both to reading aloud and silent reading.

- There is a very high percentage of words repeated. It is this skillful repetition which helps the child to read independently. Seeing words again and again, he "practices" the vocabulary he knows, and learns with ease the words that are new.

- Only 135 different words have been used, with plurals and root words counted once.

  One-half of all the words in this story have been used at least three times.

  Over one-fourth of all the words have been used at least six times.

  Some words have been used 12, 14 and 25 times.

ABOUT THIS STORY

- A dog (like a child) can be misunderstood. Loopy gets into all kinds of mischief which the humans around him just don't understand. Once you know why Loopy does what he does, his behavior, of course, is very logical. Children will not only be amused, they will also identify with this "problem" dog. They know that a child (like a dog) can be misunderstood, too!

WHAT'S THE MATTER WITH THAT DOG?

Story by MIKE MICHAELS
Pictures by RUTH WOOD
Editorial Consultant: LILIAN MOORE

WONDER BOOKS · NEW YORK

A Division of Grosset & Dunlap, Inc., New York, N. Y. 10010

Introduction

These books are meant to help the young reader discover what a delightful experience reading can be. The stories are such fun that they urge the child to try his new reading skills. They are so easy to read that they will encourage and strengthen him as a reader.

The adult will notice that the sentences aren't too long, the words aren't too hard, and the skillful repetition is like a helping hand. What the child will feel is: "This is a good story—and I can read it myself!"

For some children, the best way to meet these stories may be to hear them read aloud at first. Others, who are better prepared to read on their own, may need a little help in the beginning—help that is best given freely. Youngsters who have more experience in reading alone—whether in first or second or third grade—will have the immediate joy of reading "all by myself."

These books have been planned to help all young readers grow—in their pleasure in books and in their power to read them.

Lilian Moore
Specialist in Reading
Formerly of Division of Instructional Research,
New York City Board of Education

Library of Congress Catalog Card Number: 69-20948

Look!

A flying dog—

and a flying doghouse!

How did they get here?

The dog
and the doghouse were on a truck.
The truck went over a big bump,
and the dog and the doghouse
went flying off.

"Stop!" Danny called
to the man in the truck.
"Stop! Stop!" called Pete and Kate.
But the man in the truck
did not stop.

"What a funny dog!" said Pete.

"And what a funny house!"

said Kate. "What do the words say?"

"The words are silly," said Pete.

"No," said Danny. "Look!

The words say LOOPY'S HOUSE.

Here, Loopy! Come here!"

"Here, Loopy!" said Pete.

"Come here."

But Loopy did not come.

"Here, Loopy!" said Kate.

"Come here."

But Loopy did not come.

"What's the matter with that dog?"
said Danny.

13

Just then a mother and a baby

came by.

"Good dog!" said the mother,

and she went on.

Loopy went, too.

"No, no!" cried the mother.

"Go away!

What's the matter with that dog?"

16

"No, Loopy, no!" said Danny.

And he picked Loopy up.

A man was cutting grass.

Putt-a-putt-putt-putt-putt.

The man went around and around
cutting the grass.

So did Loopy.

He went around, too.

"Go away!" cried the man.

"Danny, take this dog away."

"No, Loopy, no!" said Danny,

and he picked Loopy up.

The ice-cream truck came

down the street.

Loopy jumped up

on the truck.

"What's the matter with that dog?"
said the ice-cream man.

"We don't know," said Danny.

"Maybe he wants some ice cream,"
said the ice-cream man.
"Here, Loopy!"

But Loopy did not want
ice cream.

Just then a girl
came out of the store.
She had bags and bags
and bags of food.

She had Loopy, too.

He jumped up

and sat

on the eggs.

"My eggs, my eggs!" cried the girl.

"See what you did!"

Loopy ran away.

Loopy ran down the street.

He saw the bus.

The bus was about to go.

Loopy jumped into the bus,
but Danny went after him
and took him off the bus
just in time.

"What's the matter with that dog?"
said the bus man.

"What is the matter with you,
Loopy?" said Kate.

"You jumped on the bus . . .

and you jumped on the ice-cream
truck . . .

and you sat on the eggs."

"What IS the matter with you,
Loopy?" said Pete.

x

36

"There he goes again," cried Danny.

"Get him, get him!" cried Pete.

Loopy went down the hill,
riding — riding,
   faster
        and faster
              and faster.

"Look out!" cried Kate.

"Look out!" cried Danny and Pete.

"Stop, stop!"

A car stopped.

So did a bus

and a fire engine . . .

and six trucks.

At last Loopy stopped, too,
right on top of a policeman.

"Is this your dog?"

the policeman asked.

"No," said Kate.

"No," said Danny.

"No," said Pete.

"Oh-ho!" said the policeman.

"This dog has no home.

He will have to come with me."

"Oh, no!" said Pete.

"Please!" said Danny,

"Please don't take him away."

"He has a home," said Kate.

"Come and see."

"Show me," said the policeman.

"See!" said Kate.

"That's not a home,"

said the policeman.

"That's a doghouse."

Just then a truck stopped.

Loopy ran and jumped

into the truck.

"Now what's the matter
with that dog?"
said the policeman.

A man jumped out of the truck.

He put Loopy's house
into the truck.

"Nothing is the matter
with my dog," he said.
"He just likes to ride

IN anything,

ON anything,

at any time.

Come on, Loopy,

Let's ride."

So Loopy went riding away.

And this time the truck

did not go over a big bump.

CHOOSE FROM THESE EASY READERS

5901 Will You Come to My Party?

5902 Hurry Up, Slowpoke

5903 Mr. Pine's Mixed-Up Signs

5904 The Adventures of Silly Billy

5905 The Secret Cat

5906 Billy Brown Makes Something Grand

5907 Miss Polly's Animal School

5908 The Duck on the Truck

5909 A Train for Tommy

5910 Surprise in the Tree

5911 The Monkey in the Rocket

5912 Billy Brown: The Baby Sitter

5913 Fly-Away at the Air Show

5914 Arty the Smarty

5915 The Surprising Pets of Billy Brown

5916 Barney Beagle

5917 I Made a Line

5918 Laurie and the Yellow Curtains

5919 Grandpa's Wonderful Glass

5920 Benjamin in the Woods

5921 Barney Beagle Plays Baseball

5922 The Day Joe Went to the Supermarket

5923 Question and Answer Book

5924 Jokes and Riddles

5925 Let Papa Sleep!

5926 The Surprise in the Story Book

5927 The Big Green Thing

5928 The Boy Who Fooled the Giant

5929 More Jokes and Riddles

5930 Too Many Pockets

5931 The Clumsy Cowboy

5932 Cat in the Box

5933 How the Animals Get to the Zoo

5934 The Birthday Party

5935 Little Gray Mouse and the Train

5936 Mr. Pine's Purple House

5937 When I Grow Up

5938 One Kitten is not Too Many

5939 How to Find a Friend

5940 The Boy, the Cat and the Magic Fiddle

5941 Little Gray Mouse Goes Sailing

5942 Keep Your Eyes Open

5945 Old Man and the Tiger

5946 Barbie Goes to a Party

5947 Barney Beagle and the Cat

5948 What's Going on Here?

5949 Little Popcorn

5951 The Fox Who Traveled

5952 The Three Coats of Benny Bunny

61